Anansi was a greedy trickster.

He cooked sweet yams for dinner.

A hungry terrapin smelled the yams.

“Can I join you for dinner?” the terrapin begged.

“Yes,” said the trickster. “But it is bad manners to have mud on your hands.”

The terrapin went to the river to get the mud off. Then he went back for dinner.

But the greedy trickster had gobbled up all the food!

The terrapin felt upset, but he had a plan.

“Visit me for lunch,” he said.

The terrapin's house was at the bottom of the river.

"I cannot get to that house without help," the trickster said to himself.

The trickster filled his jacket pockets with rocks. He jumped into the river and sank.

The trickster sat with the terrapin and licked his lips.

"It is bad manners to have a jacket on at lunch," said the terrapin.

The greedy trickster was hungry. He quickly took off his jacket.

Without the rocks, the trickster floated up and up. He dragged himself out and onto the river bank.

Dripping wet, the greedy trickster looked into the river. He had been tricked back!